4/3/13

Tracey,
    It has been such a
pleasure to work with you.
Thanks for sharing stories of
your children's escapades! ☺
Barbara

The SEASONS of LIFE

Written by BARBARA MURRAY

Illustrated by MARISSA CORBIN

PISCATAQUA

PRESS

Published by Piscataqua Press
142 Fleet Street | Portsmouth, New Hampshire 03801 | USA
603.431.2100 | info@piscataquapress.com

Printed in the United States of America

ISBN-13: 978-0-9885370-8-8

Library of Congress Control Number: 2013932657

ACKNOWLEDGMENTS

I wish to express my deepest thanks to Linda Maynard of Farmington, New Hampshire for introducing me to Marissa Corbin, who brought this poem to life with her illustrations. Very special thanks go to Diane MacPherson of Lowell, Massachusetts for her constant encouragement and support. I also want to thank Tom Holbrook of Piscataqua Press in Portsmouth, New Hampshire for making this book possible.

One **EARLY SPRING I ENTERED THE WOODS**
To see what I could find.
I had so many questions.
A lot was on my mind.

I hoped that the woods would tell me
What I wanted so much to learn.
What, after all, was the meaning of life?
Was there a plan that I could discern?

So one March day I walked down a dirt road
That led into a forest of green.
All alone I began my little search
For the answer to what does life mean.

There **WERE STILL A FEW PATCHES OF SNOW ON THE GROUND,**
Still a slight chill in the air,
But the signs of spring, the birth of the season,
Were apparent everywhere.

I followed a stream still surrounded with ice,
Slowly melting from the warmth of the sun.
I heard the stream gurgle and watched it flow
As it struggled to break free and run.

In April I heard the first chirps of birds,
As new life sprang into being.
Squirrels raced among the trees.
I marveled at all I was seeing.

Spring showers fell on tiny green buds,
Nourished by morning dew.
The woods were awash with a fragrance so sweet
As I watched all of nature renew.

Little **BUDS BEGAN TO BLOSSOM.**
Flowers began to appear.
The woods were alive and beginning to thrive
As the month of May drew near.

Now the woods were filled with music,
A delicate symphony of sound
Of chipmunks, blue jays, sparrows, and hawks
As life burst forth all around.

A yellow-eyed owl added his hoot,
A woodpecker tapped on his drum.
The music was subtle, but it was there.
I knew this was why I had come.

The meandering stream added its voice,
Now that it had been set free.
It rippled and flowed and sang with a splash
On its way to some distant sea.

I decided to continue on with my search
As the days began to grow longer.
As spring gave way to summer time,
I felt the sun grow stronger.

I Entered **THE WOODS ONE SUMMER NIGHT.**

It was in the month of June.

I meditated on this mystery

In the light of the stars and moon.

In silhouette there against the dark,
Trees arched against the night.
In silence they rose, as if on tip toes,
Piercing the sky's dark light.

They pointed to a majestic dome,
Of a blue-black vaulted sky.
The thousands of stars I saw above
Still made me question why.

I gazed at the night for quite a while,
At constellations far away,
But then I decided to continue my quest
By the light of the following day.

I saw **A WHITE-TAILED DEER AT EASE
WITH HER FAWN,**

And as June melted into July,
I watched a big moose, roaming carefree and loose.
I followed a butterfly.

I walked over every trail in the woods
Until I knew them all by heart.
I knew where I could cross the stream,
Where paths converged and broke apart.

I climbed up Sandy Hill one day.
I walked along the Cutting Trail.
I climbed Pete's Peak and observed all things
From majestic oaks to blossoms frail.

In August the woods were hot from the sun,
That filtered down through the trees,
But the piercing heat was accompanied
By a most pleasant, cooling breeze.

As **THE SUN SHOWN DOWN
UPON THE EARTH,**

Old maples offered shade.

The stream invited me to come right in,

To frolic, splash, and wade.

The woods were heavy with the scent of pine

That drifted through the air.

A soft carpet of pine needles beneath my feet

Seemed to welcome me there.

The ferns grew thick now in the woods.

Trees formed an umbrella of green.

But I must admit, I still hadn't discovered

What it could possibly mean.

The DAYS GREW SHORTER AS SEPTEMBER
Crept upon the land.
As I saw the woods changing again,
I still tried to understand

As summer slowly turned into fall,
Bright colors were splashed over trees.
Red, gold, orange, and yellow leaves
Waved vibrantly in the breeze.

I saw **SOME GEESE FLY BY ABOVE.**
They seemed to be headed south.
They flew in flocks, in V-shaped wings,
Toward a distant river's open mouth.

One day I sensed a chill in the air.
The stream began to run cold
As this brand new season, revealing a reason,
Slowly began to unfold.

Fall foliage painted the forest
As the sounds in the woods became mute.
Brilliant October seemed to be waving good-bye,
Rendering to life its final salute.

I saw a red leaf fall to the ground
On one splendid November day.
Soon it turned a very dull brown,
Decomposed and was blown away.

Then I WATCHED AS ALL THE LEAVES
Eventually fell all around.
The trees stood naked, their garments strewn
Beneath them on the ground.

I watched as death embraced the woods
In a grip held tight and firm.
I wondered if maybe from all of this
There was something I might learn.

I saw **AN OLD MAPLE TREE,
STATELY AND TALL,**

Standing leafless and so all alone.

It seemed to be crying at all of this dying,

As it stood abandoned by song birds now flown.

Some trees were now just skeletons.

The woods became barren and cold.

Death was unrelenting

In this seasonal choke hold.

North winds blew in howling gusts

Against tree limbs now so bare.

The trees stood by without defense

As death circled in icy air.

Fall gave way to winter,

While the woods looked so forlorn.

The trees stood patiently waiting,

As if longing to be reborn.

One **DECEMBER MORNING I
ENTERED THE WOODS.**
It had snowed the night before.
A cathedral of pine stood before me,
Majestic above a white forest floor.

A grand silence filled the forest now,
So strong it could not be broken.
It seemed as though in this new white dawn,
Not a word had ever been spoken.

I listened to that silent hush.
I felt a stillness so reverent and deep.
I looked all around and could not hear a sound,
As I saw that the woods were asleep.

The **FOREST HAD BEEN TRANSFIGURED**
On this beautiful winter day.
It was all recognizable and still the same,
But different in every way.

Boughs of fir trees under the weight
Of newly fallen snow,
In this brand new weather, all together,
Seemed to be bowing low.

As if praising God and thanking Him,
On this glistening brand new day,
For clothing the woods once again
In such an elegant way.

Shiny white crystals reflecting the sun
Now glistened in winter's light,
Reassuring the trees and telling the woods
That everything indeed was all right.

I entered THE WOODS ONE JANUARY DAY

During winter's afterglow.
The little stream waited in silence
Beneath the ice that capped its flow.

I walked along the Cutting Trail
That weaved among the pine.
Beneath snow so deep, I felt the woods sleep,
Waiting for winter's decline.

I climbed up Sandy Hill one morning,
As it lay wrapped in a blanket of snow.
Under a mantle of white, it slept so tight,
Its brown granules now hidden below.

In February, i climbed Pete's Peak
So I might get a better view,
And beneath me spread, gently tucked into bed,
All of nature so brilliantly new.

Nothing STIRRED AMONG THE TREES.
All was peacefully serene.
The woods were patiently waiting still
To awake from this deep winter dream.

One early spring I entered the woods
And I thought I could sense something stirring.
I heard some honey bees off in the distance,
Like an alarm clock buzzing and whirring.

And as I stood there on that fine spring day,
I believed that I understood
The reasons for seasons as they were revealed
During my time in the woods.

It was as if I came to understand,
Within the forest, God's plan for man.
The meaning of life now before me lay,
As if to the woods I heard God say ...

"Awake **ALL YOU WHO HAVE SLUMBERED SO,**
Throughout the long winter night.
Dawn is now breaking and gently awaking
The forest to new morning light.

Arise this day and go on your way.
Welcome the new morning sun.
Bear witness to My plan, My promise to man,
That death shall be overcome.

Death is but a long sleep with dreams so deep.
Time shall pass like the blink of an eye.
A new world waits to be born with the rising dawn,
As night dissolves in a sunlit sky.

Seasons, repeat your story, reveal My glory,
With your perennial themes.
In a resplendent new dawn, man shall rise and live on.
Show that this is what life truly means.

Now hear My voice, arise and rejoice,
Proclaim throughout the land,
What to man I shall say on one glorious day,
'Your resurrection is now at hand.'"

I left **THE WOODS ONE FINE SPRING MORNING.**

It was time to be on my way.

As I walked I listened, as ever so slowly,

All of nature began to obey.

CPSIA information can be obtained
at www.ICGtesting.com
Printed in the USA
LVIC041731260313
325347LV00011B

9 780988 537088